Laurie Taylor
CHANGING THE PAST

Laurie Taylor

CHANGING THE PAST

Drawings by Randall Scholes

The Minnesota Voices Project #6
New Rivers Press
1981

Copyright © 1981 by Laurie Taylor Sparer
Library of Congress Catalog Card Number: 81-83881
ISBN: 0-89823-029-2
All Rights Reserved
Typesetting: Peregrine Cold Type
Book Design: C. W. Truesdale
Author Photograph: Linette Sparer

Our thanks to the following publications in which many of these poems originally appeared: *Calliope*; *The Cape Rock*; *Cedar Rock*; *Dacotah Territory*; *Descant*; *Eureka Review*; *Greensboro Review*; *New Laurel Review*; *North Country*; *Northeast Journal*; *Samisdat*; *Sing, Heavenly Muse!*; *Southern Poetry Review*; *Storystone*; and *Webster Review*. "Stone Images" first appeared in *Cimarron Reivew* and is reprinted here with the permission of the Board of Regents for Oklahoma State University, holders of the copyright.

This book was published with the aid of grants from Dayton Hudson Foundation, Jerome Foundation, the Arts Development Fund, and the National Endowment for the Arts. This publication was also made possible by a grant provided by the Metropolitan Council from funds appropriated to the Minnesota State Arts Board by the Minnesota State Legislature.

The Minnesota Voices Project books are distributed by:

> Bookslinger,
> 330 East 9th St.
> St. Paul, MN 55101

> and

> Small Press Distribution, Inc.
> 1784 Shattuck Ave.
> Berkeley, CA 94709

CHANGING THE PAST has been manufactured in the United States of America for New Rivers Press, Inc. (C. W. Truesdale, Editor/Publisher), 1602 Selby Avenue, St. Paul, Minnesota 55104 in a first edition of 1000 copies, of which 25 have been signed and numbered by the author and the artist.

For Allen

CHANGING THE PAST

Part One: KEROSENE DREAMS

11. Kerosene Dream
12. The Man Who Perfected Medusa
13. Moon Landing
14. Lake Country
15. Almost Home Again
16. Night Terrors
17. Stone Images
18. Descendent Of Pioneers
19. Beyond Opera
20. Anaesthesia
21. Cellar Cleaning
22. "Equus" In Spring
23. A Nightmare
24. Donner Pass
25. Living With Headhunters
26. Chickens
27. Field Museum, Chicago
28. Double-Deck Solitaire
29. Diving Too Deep

Part Two: *IN CAMERA*

33. Ansel Adams
34. *In Camera*
36. Lightning-Struck Tree
37. Sunnyside Gardens
38. A Matter Of Perspective
39. Speed Skaters
40. Summer Elegy
41. Of The Order *Neuroptera*
42. Airport
43. For Sale
44. Brussels Sprouts

Part Three: CHANGING THE PAST

49. Trimming The Ivy
50. In The Water Gardens
51. Horizons
52. Medicine Wheel
53. Maimed Duck At Wood Lake
54. Wolves In Como Park
55. Tiger Sleeping In The Zoo
56. Seal Walk
57. Summer Blossoms
58. Time Capsule
61. Gift Cutting
62. Yellow Birds
64. Coming Down
65. If With My Spade
66. Crossing The Grasslands
67. Valentine
68. Suddenly The Chickadees
69. Behind the Mobil Station
70. The Big Battles On T.V.
71. Changing The Past
72. What Might Have Been

Part One: KEROSENE DREAMS

KEROSENE DREAM

Try to sleep lightly tonight:
the last roosters keep silence under the dust;
the clock is afraid of lightning.
Only the cat knows what to do.

Count up our urgencies: speak
(like the wind) only when hindered.
Step over the cat.
That thunder is only the dawn.

THE MAN WHO PERFECTED MEDUSA

The man who perfected Medusa
lies on the beach, brown as any other.
He has a wife, a child, perhaps a lover:
they know his laughter.
In the thin tendrils of his heart
the corpuscles squeeze by in orderly rows,
marching to a drum he shares with everyone.

The man who perfected Medusa
knows, but refuses to remember what he knows.
He keeps her locked in a cell
of his brain, where no surgeon's knife
could possibly free her.
Only in dreams, his scared ear recalls
how the snakes hiss, how the breeze goes still.

MOON LANDING

  So precisely imagined,
this landfall, we never were lonely
sailing our eggshell
in the sea's maze, or shoaling,
the island an absence of stars.
  Dawn is relentless:
we see, that to land here
we must pretend pretending still.
To look full turns bones to sand.
  The island resists us,
with thick roots, with rockface,
weapons used shamelessly and well.
The white beaches we had hoped for
founder.
  Yet we had thought
even of this, have long practiced
thrusting off rocks, tangling our lines
in this tangle of roots, drawing in.
The picture unspools lazily
in the mind's eye, exactly as always.
  And in the mind's eye
the future reels backward:
within the wilderness, surely, temples,
gardens hedged with bougainvillea,
just a little bit farther,
just a little while longer.

LAKE COUNTRY

I am growing used to this place.
Hills slowly manifest
in the earth's slight declines.
Peat on my trowel
no longer startles me.

I have tucked down roots
of species I never saw elsewhere.
Leaves have flourished
while my old plants grew spindly
in the long winters.

My children no longer listen.
Rock face, sand dune,
fireflies, dogwood, salt air: myths
of a woman fearful of stillness,
mindful of tides.

ALMOST HOME AGAIN

Check back. Did the sky
always lean on these hills?
—almost cozy—and did the hills
cuddle the road like this?

The road's wider, striped;
but the same trees still escort
the curves, the old reflectors
fisted in bark.

Same patch of blackberries!
Picked clean—it's nearly fall.
A minute now, and the town
will rise to meet us.

My children stare, hunting
for something of Minnesota.
The little one wants to know
if the sky is falling.

NIGHT TERRORS

This screaming, I know, does stop.
I need only bob dory-gentle
over the orange sea of your carpet
until your head rocks on my chest
and your thumb stoppers your fears.

Yet everything I've struggled to dismantle
assembles, mocked by the moon's slant grin.
I drag the echo of my thin heart,
ebb tide staining a weedy beach
where gulls dip, and fly away scandalized.

Your eyes are blank, frosted windows
acknowledging no mother. It is
as I suspected: I have strung your loom.
The warp of matted seaweed
weaves monsters with the moon's cold rays.

STONE IMAGES

They say,
in Bengali moonlight those round hips
and slender waists revolve,
though carved in stone;
the jewels flash,
the full lips part and smile;
bells at the ankles jangle, cymbals ring
between the slender fingers.
For audience,
the inhabitants of the night
slink in the temple's shadow.
For incense,
the jungle flowers yield their cloying scent.

I have my own stone images.
Under a harsh New England moon
their shadows flicker; a distant hum
escapes their tightened lips,
mice rustle at their feet—
and always,
always my throat is clogged
when the crisp incense of burning leaves
eats up the sky and beckons to the moon.

DESCENDENT OF PIONEERS

Up here there are only a few people,
loosely banded near a pair of gas pumps
marked boldface on the map.

Even in sunlight I keep to the highway.
The car is small, foreign, elderly,
unreliable;
the blackberries glow in the red lanes,
but keen-nosed bears
snuffle at the blurred edge of vision.

I'm not that woman who drove this way
with one old mule, and when the mule died
walked,
knowing wolves rule all nights.
You won't find me walking.
You won't find me glancing
at the bears.

BEYOND OPERA

In my role as Bird Snared
I was worth more to you, surely,
than whole flocks of free flyers—
hence, when I fluttered,
you clamped your stern hand
on my pinions, and yanked.

Pain enough. Still, I hummed,
dragging lopped quills
over strings of taut pages
'til you throttled my song
to a cheep, and my syrinx
distended with silence.

Then my feathers grew back! You
wanted to crack the long hollow bones
of my wings on the rack
of your logic, and bob each new note
to a quaver. Insane Papageno,
be still: this aria's mine.

ANAESTHESIA

It's an old routine:
the bored electric syllable
acknowledging the heart,
the needle-prick, the instant sleep.
People haven't the patience of beasts
with dying.
          Only once
was there a dream. Hollyhocks.
Nothing more. But whether
the dream began the sleep
or the sleep the dream
was impossible to say. Trust
the delicacy of knives,
suspend the anonymity
of wrapped faces. Sleep
begins, a cold sting
exploring its first vein:
hope for flowers, flowers
that bend in wind and trust
in bees.

CELLAR CLEANING

In the dark
above the foundation walls,
a wilderness of spider eggs
to be swept out.
Cocoons that don't bother
with metamorphosis:
a spider, shining,
kicks away each too-small skin
one leg at a time.
What you thought was an army
of dead
is only outgrown husks.
From a chink
between joist and subfloor
the living beast
watches with eight eyes
for you to leave,
as patient as a recurring dream,
as endlessly fecund.

"EQUUS" IN SPRING

Stilled, the poised hoof strains
the cocked bronze pastern
with the urge to lift. Year after year
the green ears prick
down that long alley where the elms
stealthily thicken their shade.
The oval green seeds gather
at the cracks between the paving stones,
a pattern of hexagons receding
into an unmet temptation.
Stealthily the urge to lift
overcomes the alley,
the strained bronze ears
cock toward the poised elms.
Hexagons shift at the urging
of the oval seeds. The polished green
of the pricked ears mounts
to the arched branches of the elms.
Year upon year, the hexagons recede
into that poised alley, lifting
pricked green leaves from the cracks.
Temptation. The pastern strains,
the ears stand poised, the shade daily
thickens over flanks
that seem to tremble.

A NIGHTMARE

My friend
teaches me her new method
of meditation. "Dream
meditation,"
it's called. She shows
me how to compose my limbs,
empty my mind.
I learn.
I learn far too well:
my own dreams vanish.
The only visions I can see
are hers.

DONNER PASS

Bread. Beer.
Odor of phlox
and mown grass.
Ice
is so simple an extremity.
I have been feeding on you
for years. You
would devour me,
if you could.

LIVING WITH HEADHUNTERS

Look, this spirit knows its own home,
inhabited so many years (though larger then,
the hair not quite so thick).
It likes this boiled house,
strange and familiar all at the same time.
It took so long to get comfortable in it—
but the one room no longer changes. Dust
collects in the nostrils, the eye holes
are missing something.

Yet it will make the best of it.
That's just a new sort of human condition,
that tight scalp, the brainpan shivered
the hot sand lodged in its place.
People put up with stranger indignities:
even the Sibyl, squatting on her dry
immortal haunches, wore out her curses
and plays mumbledypeg on the grainy beach
with an old cuttlebone.

CHICKENS

—brush drawing, anonymous Japanese

On a lighter part
of the paper, hooks
and spikes of black
shadow feathers.
Should they have wattles?
Good. A blotch
of pale red, then the brush returns
with black: eyes, beaks,
as quickly as the hand
can scratch.
            In Arizona,
the air turns all sun.
Millions
of white chickens escape their coops,
bulldozed under
the baked earth.

Ten chickens
in a Japanese yard
crowd one corner
of the wide page,
free.

FIELD MUSEUM, CHICAGO

:ghost dance: :shell game:

Yesterdays shelled in glass
the quilled and beaded shells
of men   Danced
on sweating bodies, urged
the good hunt's return

turn the baskets:empty
years have stunned the land
into squares, have danced the men
away in parentheses
of buffalo print, enclosed

closing time. Bronze valves
swing to the mantle of steps
up and down, people in patterns
threshing their sorrows
out of their yesterdays

DOUBLE-DECK SOLITAIRE

Two kinds of cards
to be considered here.
the green-backed deck
displays a ship, three-masted,
just enough topsail struck
to show the solidness of storm.
Surely these sailors believe
a man's breath makes more dint
in wind than the wing
of any gull, surely they care nothing
for anchors, whether iron
or canvas! The orange back
of the other deck
could be delight or warning,
and a ship
with every scrap of sail set
heaves out of the bright clouds
on an indigo sea. Such ships
lean after brass-bound compasses
soothed in gimbals, take sight
on the constancy of stars.

The game deals all the cards
face-up, requires only
that one threat a path
between luck and rules
to sort the suits. Red and black
slip pip-by-pip
into eternity. No way of knowing
which ship booms in the wind,
which wind is blowing.

DIVING TOO DEEP

We fall for it every time:
the illusion of clear water,
the imagined gold
passive among gelatinous frills—
no guards here. Just
these embodied fantasies,
mute feeding creatures
stalked to their forefathers—
What will they care about our fingers
searching among them?

So. We plunge. Fish
dart unheeded warnings;
the frills hastily withdraw.
Outdiving the beaded string of air
that ties us to our time,
our downstretched hands shear toward bottom:
the gold eludes us after all.

Beached, cramped, exhausted;
the once-lithe body petrified,
the eloquent tongue
reduced to a list of pains—
this memory quickly fades. In time,
we struggle erect, ready to dive again,
crazy as ever.

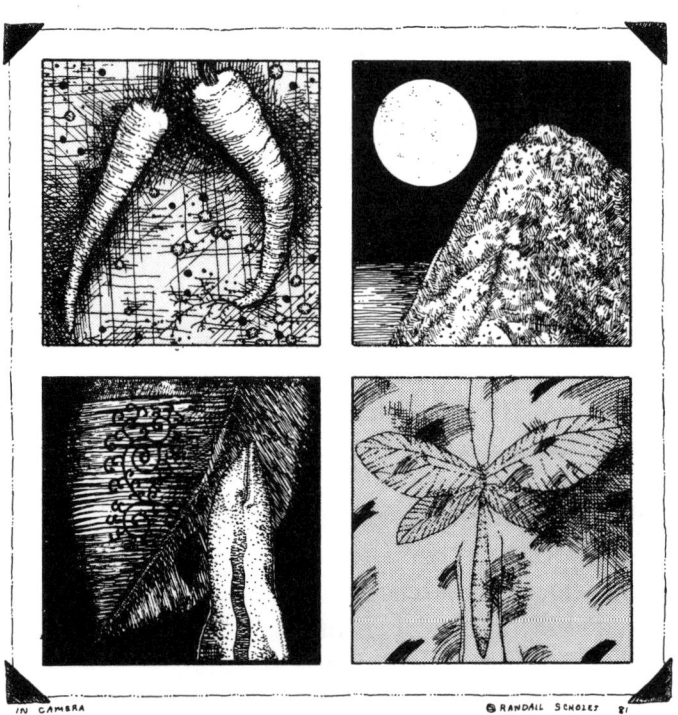

IN CAMERA © RANDALL SCHOLES 81

Part Two: *IN CAMERA*

ANSEL ADAMS

Nothing so chancy or bizarre
that no one will try it.
Stop the moon
from rolling down the sky.
Render a waterfall
a marvel of failed inertia,
root sheep
as solidly as lettuces.

A mayfly
could achieve eternity
in a world like this—
as delicately silted as a fern
or trilobite, its ability to fly
mere inference, like those other selves
that stare at us
out of childhood snapshots.

IN CAMERA

I carried my three lenses
into this wind, this hodgepodge
of berries and brilliant leaves,
water and sky, sun and red reflections.
The wood, the field, the stream mingle
in a series of pictures as I step forward,
drawn by the hot colors the way solder
flows toward heat along its fluxed path.
Like solder, I harden the moment's jostle
into good order.

Oh, I'm an old hand at picture-smithing.
No need to tame the world
in the crossed gnomons of fingers and thumbs.
My camera's a finger-snap,
a reflex of my mind's eye; now,
though I've tried to be judicious,
it hangs at my side, replete.

As I rest, nimble sparrows
angle in squadrons for the seedheads
bowing beside the stone wall. The sky's twinkle
through wind-brushed leaves, the bubble
of the sun along clear water,
the graceful bend of foxtail,
lie fixed in the instants of my camera's eye,
and thereby are lost—

or only altered: any new mind supplying
loft to the suspended wing, swirl
to the moired surface of the stream.
But the wing will not cant again,
the stream never brighten,

and even I may never see this field
except as if stopped, cropped,
annealed to a new working, its whisper
forever in another tongue.

Eagerness is part of any craft.
But even in my haste to polish, I linger
at my standpoints, to look again—
here's the dark pool where a huge log
muffles the stream. And here
is where I stood to frame that maple,
garnet now, when the sun heated its leaves
until the color flowed into the water,
flooding against the log—

But the sun has dropped. Now
I also see the red leaves floating
on the stilled water, an armada
each with a different draft, the ribs of each
sprung in different curves, each hoisting
its own colors. But it's almost dark,
and there's no film left.

LIGHTNING-STRUCK TREE

It all happened so fast! Yet
how time dragged on my eye:
an endless flash,
slow bark ribboning
clear to the root, and the grass
leaping above the rootpaths....

In that crack of deafness,
time to recollect. Orioles.
Bamboo rakes. A woman
in a lavender dress, holding
a small child to the camera.

The odor of singed wood
permeates the air.
From the heartwood,
steam uncoils, like a ghost.

SUNNYSIDE GARDENS

Southeast,
jagged flags of rain.
Under thousand-breasted clouds
the long tables of flowers
brighten. Women
hurry between calico rows
of pansies,
hauling wagonfuls
of new garden.
The rain swoops down,
drenching newspaper rainhats,
cars, plastic-bagged
manure. But the poppies,
the marigolds,
burn, burn.

A MATTER OF PERSPECTIVE

In this neutral light
we find the delusion of clarity
of old lithographs.
The houses all seem bluff
and upright, the scarves bright,
although the spruces
are pleated by snow.

Could the hill tumble?
It springs so steeply
at the horizon! Slick
along the edges of the street
cars drawn by unseen horses
slip white-eyed downward
and tremble at its base.

It's all a matter
of perspective. Mr. Currier
counts the years
the hill has held; Mr. Ives
assures us all, the scarves
will be bright, the houses staunch,
the trees erect—
until the light changes.

SPEED SKATERS

in brilliant skins
swoop down the lens:
a good skater keeps her feet
beneath her. Offers no body
to the wind. But
to flee what,
jaw set forward?
Or pursue what, one hand
tucked behind?
The camera backs up:
they are almost upon it,
they have flushed it
high into the air!
But the wing beats
belong to the skaters,
hawks stooping, can it be?
Only upon their own old track?

SUMMER ELEGY

Eloquent singer in the shadowed sea,
shadow himself, swirler
of fiery motes that mark his passage
in glides of light, the blue whale hums
his lone presence in the ocean's ear.

How time drives
this sounder of deep water
to his last bright polar summer!

Oiler of watches, softener of boots,
feeder of cats and of corn—
these still wait
in the pain, the last plunge, the red
dismemberment in the frozen air.

OF THE ORDER *NEUROPTERA*

A lacewing has taken refuge
from the cold, up there,
at the corner of ceiling and wall
where the furnace-air lodges.
A lacewing, for all its bright eyes,
is useless (the garden book says)
but its larvae eat aphids,
and cleverly creep about
with old skins and excrement
piled on their backs, a means
of concealment. Think of poems
trying to survive long enough
to fly, and wonder what the words
are hiding.

AIRPORT

Dusk. The giants sleek,
tended like insect queens
brooding above the workers.

In the plate glass
our world and theirs mingle:
a pinball machine
lights the pilot's console,
ceiling lights trace runways,
trucks race through waiting people
as if through ghosts.

Impossible to sort it out
while sitting here.
Turn your back,
or stand close, peering
through your own shadow.
You'll see clearly then, but
only what you choose.

FOR SALE

In the shop window, a tumble of arms
and plaster breasts: above the bald,
chipped heads a sign
with the phone number.

Who would want to buy
these women, lopped at the waist
and standing,
as if on streetcorners,
with steel shafts
already in place?

Sisters, your eyes, so open
to the future, astound me!
I salute your panache:
how elegant you are!
How unconcerned!

Is it vanity that buoys you?
Or just the relief
of being naked in a shop window,
admitting you've been dismembered,
admitting that you're for sale?

BRUSSELS SPROUTS

Snapped
from the lordly
leaning stems
(my aphid-smeared thumb
protesting November)
the last crop
of this season.
Only stragglers
—a leek, three carrots,
some frost-nipped lettuce—
left from warmer weather.
The poems
of young men are sweet,
like new peas, and those
of the mature
juicy as tomatoes,
as melons,
earthy
as string beans. Sprouts
have tooth to them,
and keep
all winter.

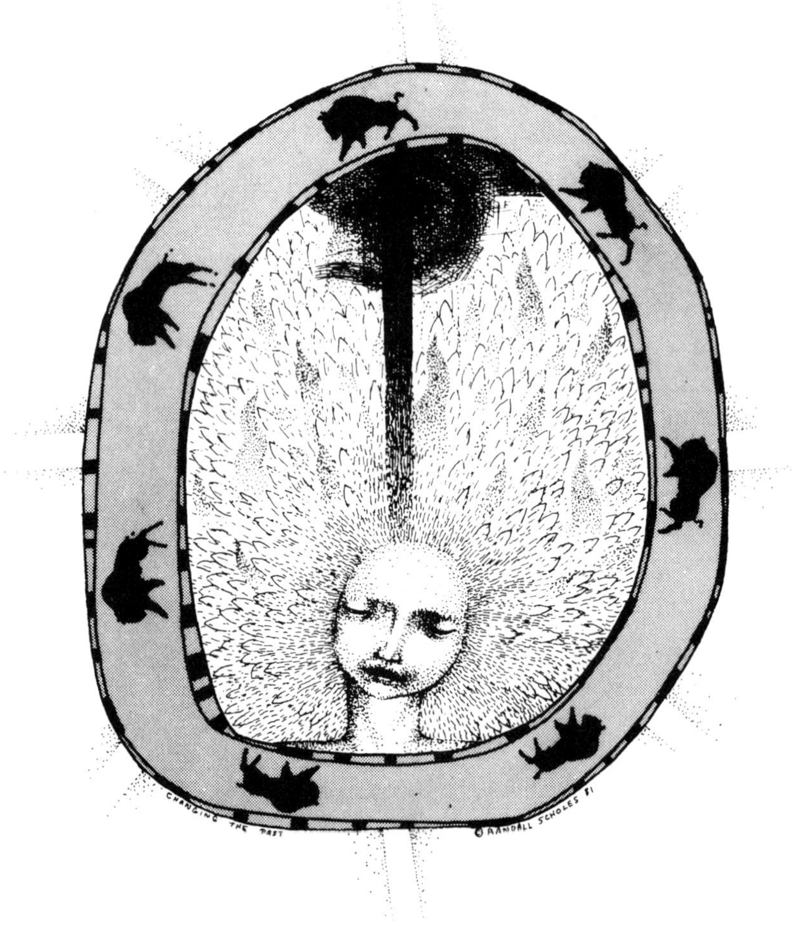
CHANGING THE PAST
© RANDALL SCHOLES 81

Part Three: CHANGING THE PAST

TRIMMING THE IVY

Each fall you thrust the ladder
throught he chimney vines, and each fall I
stand on the bottom rung for weight.

There you are, blotted at the other end
of the aluminum rise—heels lapping calves,
calves lapping thighs, thighs your bent ass

and nothing above that but the blue clouds
scudding toward winter. But I can't look up:
stems torn from the chimney mouth rattle down

and the red leaves come twirling earthward
for the cat to chase. Each year the birches
mount higher on the sky. The vines grow thick.

IN THE WATER GARDENS

Leaning over the flaking bark
of the bridge rail,
I caught the ungainly pods
of lotus in two hands,
held, for a moment,
Egypt,
India,
distant China, all
those mysterious
unreachable lands.

Thirty years
and fifteen hundred miles away
I'm told
the man who kept the water garden
was the father
of my mother-in-law's old friend.

With such small linkages
strangers can pass letters hand-to-hand,
reaching an unknown man in Australia
in just three weeks.

HORIZONS

The old men stake the first gleam
at the rim of the frozen sky
to know when the leash is most strained
and the sun must sigh back.
Now comes the deep ice:
the fires snapping at terror,
the children in hunger.
The old men count the dawn notches
on the calendar bones
and promise spring. The mothers
know better; they shelter each spark
with their hearts;
they measure their laughter.

MEDICINE WHEEL

Take this circle of unassuming stones:
in its youth it clocked the stars
in their slant wheel, and told those
who knew its reading when to plant
or harvest, when to move on.

Untended, forgotten all these years
since they did move on,
it lies under that same drift of stars,
blind, dumb; calm as the brown circle
under the proud spruce boughs.

MAIMED DUCK AT WOOD LAKE

Safe, enclosed
in the new familiarity of woven wire,
she must live
over and over and over
the horror of the severed wing.
She will eat
but never preens.

Rising from the reeds
of the calm lake, her flock heads south,
calling through the sunset.

In the pink light of her cage
she echoes their raucous chatter
with the mew of a tired child.
She must know better now
than to try to follow.

She stoops to the dish of corn.

WOLVES IN COMO PARK

Snow dimpled by their hard round toes
inside the fence—broad impatient paths
smeared with blood.

Three dark but frosted, one lighter,
glide from the trees as if I'd knocked
and take their stations.

Maybe I've come at feeding time. Maybe
no one else comes on days this cold
without bringing meat.

The light one yawns. Eight pale eyes
question mine: a minute, maybe more,
intent as stone they measure me.

I feel my answer flow. The woods
instantly absorb the wolves. I walk on,
wondering what I've said.

TIGER SLEEPING IN THE ZOO

The child points out my twitching paws
and says I dream of blood, but I

am dreaming green:
green leaves that gleam
jeweled in rain in afternoon;
and algal green
of creeping streams;
green smells of humid soil, of trees
that fountain into air—
Oh, green, green,
that dyed my eyes
and followed me through half the world
through countless years,
I cannot wash you out with tears.
Tigers go dry of eye to sleep,
barred behind bars,
observed,
but dreaming green.

SEAL WALK

The weather has verged upon delicious
three whole days. Trees become excited
and shed their clothes.
                        The seals
tramp over their rocks on awkward feet,
puff up their whiskers:
they've guessed—the crowd,
THREE keepers, the grinning door—
barking,
it feels a little like the edge
of the long ocean, why does it lead
to that skimpy pond
with its four-o'clock fish?
                            The TV man
rattles his heartfelt warmth
in his trousers pocket. He has fifteen seconds
to persuade us of happiness
in winter quarters.

SUMMER BLOSSOMS

This summer the aspidistra bloomed.
She couldn't help herself; it was
those sensuous spathes of calla,
flaunted beside her, that were her undoing.
Still, all those years in the stays
of the prim Victorian jardiniere will tell:
dreaming of a white splendor, shame-faced,
she pushed a clumsy purplish mass
only half out of the soil, close to the rim
of her sensible pot.

TIME CAPSULE

in a coffeehouse called No Exit
the tin ceiling's painted brown
a blond guitarist sings
old Dylan songs

Back home it's 1980, but tonight
I'll be staying here with you
a little while, as if
resting legs weary with marching
for peace
or clean water

the waitress swings
her waistlong hair
sorry, they're out of mu tea
everything's
in motion—on the wall
a faded medicine drum
bumps in the stir
of the ceiling fan, fluttering
ineffectual feathers
the trees beyond the window
paddle against an ignorant wind
that seems to come
from no particular direction
the window is framed
with pathos vines
dead in their macrame

friends, you seem all
at the wrong end of the telescope,
dropping echoes that lean
against dusty brown walls

somewhere inside me
I know all the words
but the hum won't come   tonight
no light will shine
on me   years, years,
and still I see
no exit

BUSINESS TRIPS

You are already flying away
when I trace you through the silent house:
stepping in the cold footprints of your shower,
letting the cat in, reheating the coffee.

This time I heard the cab come,
beating sunrise; fragments of your voice,
the driver's; doors slamming—
sounds that eased me into your bedhollow
to wait for the alarm to ring.

Tonight our distance-wearied voices
will string the day's small miseries
on the long shining wires,
count the nights remaining, say goodnight,
leaving the conversation good as new.
Other people are waiting to use these words:
other husbands in bland plastic rooms,
other wives.

GIFT CUTTING

This plant came into my kitchen
without name or roots, utterly confident,
asking only for a drink of water,
Please, like a small child.

It is endearing,
the way it spurted roots,
filling the proffered jar,
and grasps incessantly at the light
with those small five-fingered leaves.

But it grew no name.
Somewhere, some drab-backed book
is hiding the name: a name delicate,
lovely as the fuzzed starry leaves,
snowflake lace, tiny hands
thrusting into each corner
of its pane of glass—

Among my damp chores the name
is my humming speculation. Clearly,
it has no need of names. But I,
I need the name.

YELLOW BIRDS

I

Suddenly I remember that my grandmother
(that stern-mouthed woman)
once kept a canary. Oh,
I am sure of it!
I can see the bird now,
the pale eastern sun on its feathers,
hopping from perch to perch
in its round cage.
And didn't she also tune the radio
to the program
where the Hartz Mountain Canaries
warbled along with the music?
All in hope that her bird
would join in, all that trilling,
all that spilling of joy!
But the bird never sang.

II

Ah, and the canaries
in that hotel in Patras!
Grade Epsilon, and no pretensions.
Scuffling from bed to toilet
one passed through the *stoa*,
and there,
hung in each archway,
a cage of canaries sang
to the red geraniums below.
How the geraniums crackled, how the birds
took fire! And all tended
by a red-haired woman
with a withered leg,
whose vibrant voice

seemed to have stolen extra life
from her flaccid muscles—
or was it that she'd learned
the canaries' way of holding
nothing back?

III

A mew at the screen door.
My cat, with a mouthful
of wild canary. He dips his head
and drops the mangled body at my feet.
Instantly
the air chills. I cannot find my voice
to chide him.

COMING DOWN

The two old ladies
call their cousin east:
"Sam, the heat won't work,
the apartment is icy,
the landlord needs yelling."
This though their brother
lives just one floor
above their heads.
They're mad at him,
they don't speak. The reason?
Gone, years ago:
the years themselves
are reason enough.
The two old ladies purse their lips
against his name: "Sam,
don't say it, Sam."
Their nostrils flare
in unison. Ah, but....

Each has her stairwell secret:
"Fannie, don't tell Gert,
I have a pin of Momma's,
here, for you, hide it."
"Gert, shh, is Fannie coming?
A good picture of Poppa,
such a nice frame, silver,
you should have it."
Sam harangues the landlord
on the telephone,
snores on the green plush couch.
The sisters dream,
the same icy dream:
each has caught the other
on the stairs,
coming down.

IF WITH MY SPADE

If I violate the earth with my spade,
in hope of flowers, if,
with my spade, I attempt
a cornucopia, if I violate, it is
life-giving penetration,
to make of earth myself,
bearing vegetables,
succulences and cracklings
like the poems I cannot make if,
with my spade, I turn my soil
delicately, fearing violation,
fearing those fruits that fall
from my hand, oozing juice
and small hovering bees
and are not mine.

CROSSING THE GRASSLANDS

The grass spills like a colorless sea
over the horizon's lip: here
there is no jetty of familiar trees
to hinder flow. The blackened hawk
aloft in the high hot wind
circles and dips, but never dives.
This sea slakes nothing.

Nor does the chittering
of small birds disturb the steady hiss.
the pliant stems have forgotten
even the rabbits. If the hawk cries,
his bugle spirals into blue
without touching ground.
The traveller is pierced with fear

that the basin may tilt, the near
edge of the earth rise, pouring
everything after the grass. Yet
there is no going back: behind,
the grass streams toward him, driving
all thought before it. Not so much
as a bone to stumble over—

only the sibilant grass and its whisper:
shall he let it flood over his head,
accepting so fickle a shade
until the sun flickers out?
Or follow, in his slow human way,
until the horizon ridges under his feet,
to watch the grass leap free?

VALENTINE

for Allen

There never were any dragons.
The White Knight has ridden away
in the clangor of a thousand tin cans.
The wind remains, to put a back to.
Mount the long red bus
and take your pencils to the tourney ground.
Joust if you must,
but come home whole.
The White Knight in his armor
never felt his lady's beating heart.

SUDDENLY, THE CHICKADEES

Suddenly, the chickadees
call *Sigfried, Sigfried.*
The flickers
whet their swords. Lilacs.
This can only be May.

The earth in the yard
is dry as flour. The white tangle
of the bellflower's roots
lifts easily free: maze
of love. Any part
could nourish any other, any
regenerate the whole.

Come-come-come-come-come,
the flickers cry.
Copulation is for beasts
that fly alone,
hunting roots. Come.

BEHIND THE MOBIL STATION

Behind the Mobil station
the creek widens, becomes
an arm's reach of water
filled with green ribbons
yearning after the current,
where dark fish hide.
A killdeer
leans and leans in the breeze,
screaming, "Where? Where?"
as if lost.

The bus comes.
The bus carries away
the black girl with corn-rowed hair
in precise pink bows,
the old lady in her flowered shift
and sneakers, and me,
naked in shirt and jeans.

THE BIG BATTLES ON T.V.

This, watch this, this
could be where Daddy
got lost.
        In that box
with the grey run-again movie.
In that plane stumbling
down a grainy sky, ending
in the usual grey flash.
                NO,
he never did that. Fetched
tin cans over and over
the grey ocean, waiting
for the nervous tin can
that never came.
              Yes,
his face turned grey, but
they shaved his cheeks
real nice and put a flower
in his buttonhole.
              That
was just thirty years after
his body marched home
and he didn't.

CHANGING THE PAST

Our knowledge now being more precise,
we can say, this happened: former historians
who trusted the contemporary account
were led astray,
the account having been provoked
by greed, guilt, ambition,
and a spiteful desire to mislead
oncoming generations—and was besides
mistaken.

As for myself, all these poems
are cast and recast until the glance
whose arc I could not plot
becomes the words I used to calculate;
the shape of a smile
fades to the letters on a page.
I cannot tell you what was real
and what interpreted, even yesterday,
or whether the thumb that left
this moth-print on my lip
was yours or mine,
or when.

History is scholarly fiction,
and poetry may be
chant or rant of human perversities.
Can you really believe
in all those drums, spears, spoons,
parchment deeds and kohl-rimmed eyes,
or that I loved you then?
Look, I show you
only the museum of a smile.

WHAT MIGHT HAVE SPOKEN

Yesterday
eased overnight from the sand,
a lacework of wavelap
left in its place—not that I thought
I'd find so much as the pool
of a heel.   The sea offers little
the honor of record: a drilled shell,
a sea urchin's test, the useless floats
of some limp weeds, what was once
a crab's right claw. Nothing else to read
but cloud-scribbled sky,
wind-scrawled water: careless runes
with no interpreters but a few coots
that nod and bow,
saying nothing.   What might have spoken
is gone in the night:
bird-cry or surf-purl,
the print of a heel—
sand dollar light in my pocket,
mandala, mandala,
crumbling to dust.
Nothing now to save or to spend.

Laurie Taylor

1-4-86

PS
3570
A9.43   Taylor, Laurie.
C4   Changing the past.
1981

NORMANDALE
COMMUNITY COLLEGE
9700 France Avenue South
Bloomington, Minnesota 55431

DEMCO